To Ishaan and Kiran, with love ~
TK

To Lucy and Harry, my very own adventure ~
SW

First published in 2012 by Scholastic Children's Books
Euston House, 24 Eversholt Street
London NW1 1DB
a division of Scholastic Ltd
www.scholastic.com
London ~ New York ~ Toronto ~ Sydney ~ Auckland
Mexico City ~ New Delhi ~ Hong Kong

Text copyright © 2012 Timothy Knapman
Illustrations copyright © 2012 Sarah Warburton

HB ISBN 978 1407 11522 1
PB ISBN 978 1407 11523 8

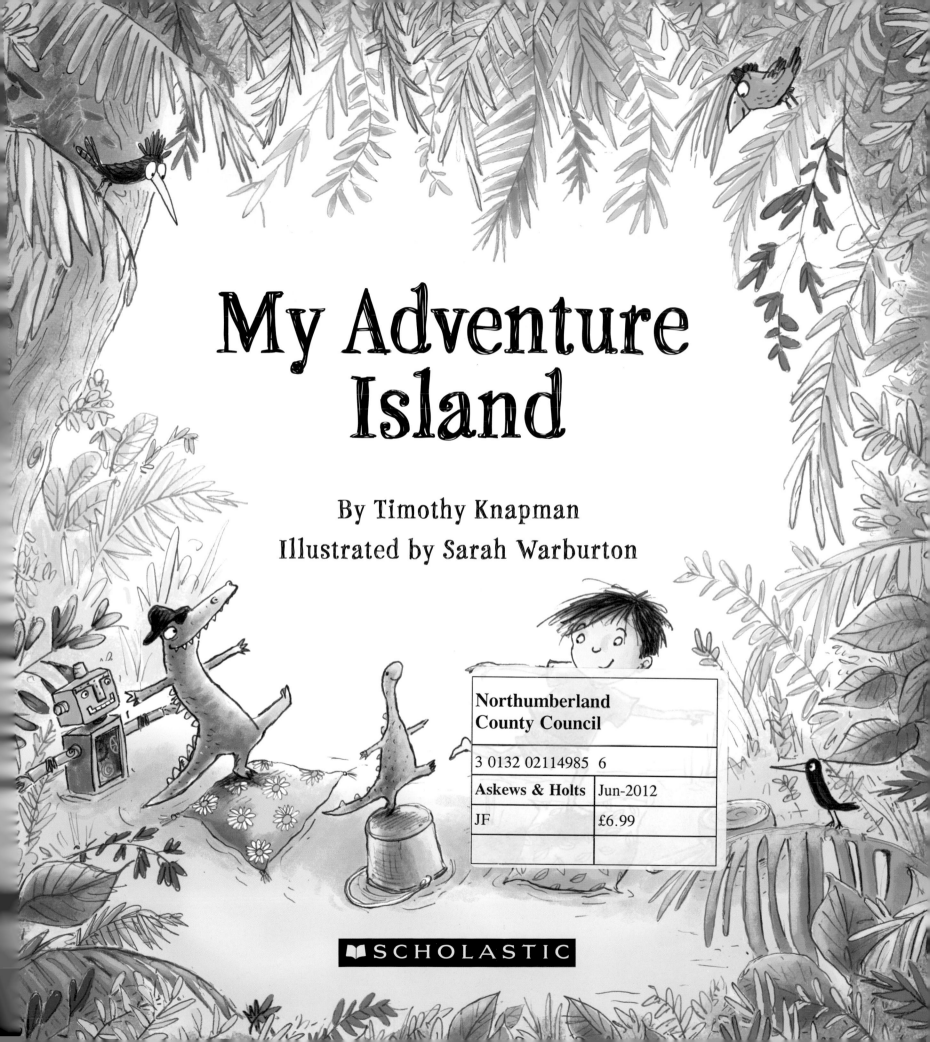

My Adventure Island

By Timothy Knapman

Illustrated by Sarah Warburton

SCHOLASTIC

Here on my island I do what I like.

I can **ZOOM** all around
on my brilliant new bike.

I can eat chocolate cake,

with cream poured on thick,

And marshmallow trifle

which **won't** make me sick.

I get all of the biggest,
most wonderful toys
Which I **don't** have to share
with the rest of the boys.

a wizard,

a knight.

I'm brave and I'm strong and I win every fight!

Here on my island
I do as I please.

I splash in the puddles
and climb all the trees.

I swing through the branches,
I fly through the sky...
And I end up face down
in a **massive** mud pie!

So what if my clothes are all dirty and torn?
How else would you know
that they'd ever been worn?

Here on my island
we don't have shampoos.
I won't have a bath
for a month if I choose.

Brushing your teeth
is just silly, I think.
And as for my feet –
what a wonderful stink!

Here on my island I stay up all night.
Having **bedtimes** for boys
can never be right.

(Though I have to make **sure** that I've turned on the light.)

Here on my island, big sisters are **banned**
And cabbage and broccoli too - which is grand!

And if you don't like it, you don't have to stay.
I'll let my pet dinosaur chase you away!

Here on my island I watch telly all day.

And I play and I play

And I PLAY and I PLAY!

I'm king of the castle,
and I say what goes,
From sticking your tongue out
to picking your nose!

It's great when you don't have
to do as you're told...

But sometimes my island
gets terribly cold.

There's no one to cuddle, or give you a kiss
Or tell you a story, and that's what I miss.

It's why, when I'm sitting
alone on the sand...

I'm glad that my island's
so close
to the land!